Super Cute Coloring Book

HELLO and WELCOME to
Super Cute Coloring
by Blue Jewel Books

HAVE A SUPER FUN TIME!

We create our books with great love and care yet mistakes beyond our control can happen in printing, binding and shipping. If you have any questions, comments, concerns, or problems with this book please contact us at: bluejewelbooks@gmail.com.

SMILE

Made in United States
Troutdale, OR
07/13/2024

21207255R00060